The Frog in the Well

Written by
Stephen Rickard

Illustrated by
Emma Hildreth

A long time ago there was a little frog.
He lived at the bottom of a deep, dark well.

The frog had insects to eat and cool, clear water to drink.

In the daytime he looked up at the blue sky and at night he looked up at the stars and the bright moon.

He was a very happy frog.

But sometimes birds flew low
and shouted down to him.

"Come up here, little frog.
Come and see the big, wide world.
It is so pleasant."

"No, thank you," said the frog.
"I am very happy down here in my well.
Come down and visit me.
You can see how nice my deep, dark well is."

But no birds went down to see the frog.

And soon the birds got fed up with the frog. He would not go up to see the wide world.

Then one day a little yellow bird flew down into the well and picked the frog up.

The bird lifted the frog on a stick and flew up, out of the deep, dark well.

"How bright things are," said the frog.
"It is too bright for me.
Look, what is that big, blue thing?
And what is that tall, white thing?
And what are the shimmering, green things?"

"They are trees," said the bird.
"The blue thing is the sea – and the big, white thing is a huge mountain. Aren't they wonderful?"

"Let me down!" said the frog.

So the yellow bird flew down to the ground and the frog hopped off.

And yes, the birds were right.

The world was wonderful! The frog enjoyed it so much.

The frog had been very happy
in his old, deep, dark well,
but he did not go back to see it again.